Otter Ground

An Aqualand Book

Parker Leckie

 The Publishing Shop

Petrolia, Ontario, Canada

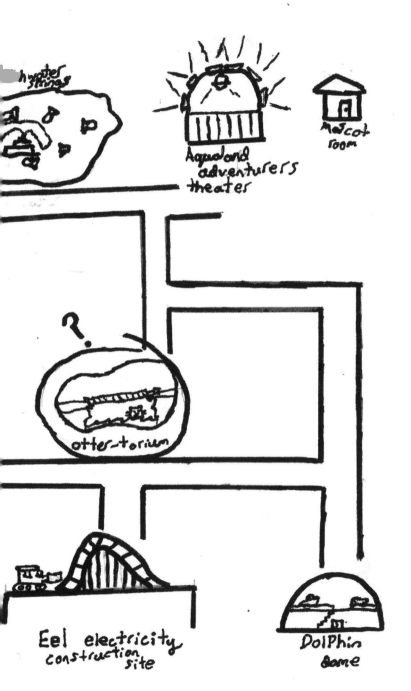

Otter Ground

ISBN: 978-1-998290-08-6

Book Design by Dawn Stilwell, The Publishing Shop

Big thanks to my friends Cameron McPhail, Lochlan Irwin, and Nathaniel Ardell who made some suggestions.

Thanks to my parents who helped my book improve a whole lot, and for believing in me the whole time.

Also, thanks to my 6th grade teacher Stefany McCallum, who inspired me to write this book.

Thanks to Ryker McDonald, who was my biggest competitor in writing.

I couldn't have made this possible without the Publishing Shop as well.

Chapter 1: Shark Bite

I found out about the stolen sea otters a bit before some sharks tried to eat me.

I was heading back home from Canada's biggest aquarium; Aqualand, to the rundown trailer park where I lived when I heard the scream. It came from Shark Shallows which was odd. You may think that it would be normal to hear a scream because there were sharks and the sharks would scare the tourists, but that wasn't the case. Sharks aren't big hunters; in fact, most shark attacks are accidental. Only ten people die due to sharks every year. (Meanwhile, one hundred fifty people die from falling coconuts.) It was just like thinking that living in Canada's biggest aquarium would be one thrill ride after another.

Aqualand was founded by the multi-millionaire Aiden River. When he heard that my mom was a fish expert and my dad was an expert photographer, he asked if they wanted a job. My parents said 'yes' and we ended up living in Aqualand, but after a few weeks, the excitement of being there faded. I had to resort to pranks for entertainment. Honestly, it was kind of pathetic that I had to paint turtle shells pink for my amusement. So, with that, being curious and seeking excitement, I ran over to Shark Shallows.

Or, at least, I tried to, I only made it a few steps before someone grabbed my arm. I spun around to find Mary Shannon, or as I liked to call her, Mad Mary. She was big, round, and dangerously smelly, especially up close. Since the day I came to Aqualand, she had been a constant thorn in my shoe, which I responded to like any other twelve-year-old; I played pranks. I did things like putting beavers in her office or replacing her olive, egg, and tuna sandwich with raw fish. (In my defense, I made it better, so she might as well be thanking me.)

"So, Jake, running from the scene of the crime I see," she sneered. "I'm onto you."

"Onto what? What did I do?" I asked. "Wait, is this about the commotion at Shark Shallows?"

She gave me a blank look. Apparently, Mad Mary hadn't heard about or seen in this matter the lump of people stationed outside of Shark Shallows.

"No, I'm talking about you making the otters disappear."

Now, that was surprising, but I still wanted to see what the problem at Shark Shallows was first. I slipped free of Mad Mary's grasp and sprinted toward the shark tank.

By the time I got there, the tourists had been mostly cleared out, so I had a perfect view of the shark tank. Shark Shallows was a giant glass dome that had hundreds of sharks in it. It gave you the sort of vibe that the sharks were circling around you. The sharks had never tried to attack anyone for two reasons.

The surrounding glass stopped them from going after tourists; the sharks noticed the glass and tended to find that the tourists would be tough prey to get to (and that's only if sharks ate humans). If a shark eats a human, it tends to spit it right out. Although once I entered, I witnessed the impossible.

The sharks were trying to get to the tourists and eat them. Of course, not all of the sharks were going after them. There were at least six of them still roaming the tank.

A sudden gasp arose from the tourists followed by a collection of shrieks. The sharks had opened their terrifyingly toothy mouths. And then all at once, the sharks pointed themselves toward me. Each beady eye watched me intently. I stood there, watching the sharks for at least a minute. After a long pause, Mad Mary rushed in. Her face was red and covered in sweat even though it was only a thirty-second jog. It seemed like it was the most exercise she had done in a year. When she entered, it took her a few seconds to comprehend what was happening, but when she did, her jaw dropped. Security's job is to make sure that no situations break out. This was a situation, but Mad Mary just stood rooted to the spot, surrounded by chaos, mouth hanging open.

Not far away, the actor dressed as Sally Shark shifted from foot to foot unsure what to do. He seemed to be deciding whether or not to abandon his post or stay in place and continue to scare little kids who were under the impression that he was a real shark.

I walked over to him and said, "You should get out of here."

The costumes were designed with a slant in the mouths to help make sure that the actors didn't knock over small children, so when I approached, he couldn't tell if I was an adult or not.

"Are you from security?" He asked.

"Yes, now get out of here." I ordered.

"Yes sir," he said and scrambled away.

I winced; some people have way too much respect for authority.

As I was watching him trip over multiple different things, someone grabbed my shoulder from behind and growled in my ear, "Who gave you permission to dismiss the actors?"

I turned around to see Blake Morris, the head of security, and said, "Well someone had to, seeing as Mary has gone brain-dead."

He glanced at Mary who snapped to attention and tried to seem as though she was doing something important. Matteo Deakin, one of the shark trainers, walked over thinking I was being accused of angering the sharks.

"Hey, if you're accusing Jake of making the sharks angry, he didn't." Matteo said.

"How do you know that?"

"Because he wouldn't have known how to do it."

"Hey!" I protested.

"Not many adults could figure out how to make a shark angry at humans, let alone a kid." Matteo said as though it was obvious, "And while I am concerned about the sharks, I don't think it's that big of a problem; that glass is meant to withstand shark attacks."

Blake, who suddenly wanted to end the conversation, turned to me and said, "You should go home."

"Fine."

I took one last look around the room and noticed something. The sharks were trying to attack me.

Chapter 2: Depressed Otters

I knew Mom would kill me if I was late for dinner, but I still wanted to see what was going on at the Otter-torium.

The Otter-torium was a large pond that had a viewing platform going through the middle of it. At certain times Aqualand would put on a show and let the otters perform. Hence the word otter-torium. Aqualand had twelve sea otters out of the three thousand left in the world. Sea otters were hunted for their fur from 1741 to 1911, which dropped their population drastically. At one point in history, they dropped to near extinction with a range of about 100-200 left. After that, they became an endangered species.

Aqualand having twelve sea otters was legendary. In retrospect, I should have been more concerned about them but at the time, I was worried about the sharks. By the time I arrived, it was dawn, past closing time, which is when most animals were active. (Zoos and aquariums open and close at the worst times possible, during the day.) When I arrived at the otter exhibit, I immediately realized something was wrong. Otters are usually active and playful but today they just floated on their backs. They were all split up too. When otters sleep, they sleep in twos. They cuddle to keep warm. Otters are extremely social to their kind, so it was odd to see them being anti-social. I counted them and ended up with five. They really were disappearing. I would have kept investigating but it was getting dark out and I didn't want to test my mom's patience, so I decided to head home.

I didn't try to sneak into the trailer for two reasons: one, the walls in our trailer were paper thin so Mom could probably hear me stomping along from half a mile away and two, our trailer is so small that you can't sneak in. The trailer was made up of three rooms: my room, my Mom and Dad's room, and everything else. So, when I walked through the door I was immediately ambushed by Mom. My mom, dad, and I used to live on a boat in the middle of a coral reef on the Pacific Ocean. My mom would study the fish while my dad took pictures. Sadly, we were forced out of that life when the US government wanted to build a military base there. (I couldn't figure out why they didn't just do it somewhere else. The coral reef isn't the only place in the ocean.)

When Aqualand said that my mom could study the fish and my dad could take photographs, they jumped at the chance. (My dad wasn't home at the moment; he was taking pictures of blue whales in the Atlantic Ocean for Aqualand at the moment.)

"Where have you been?" she asked.

"At the otter and shark exhibit."

There was no point in lying as I knew she would see right through it.

"What were you doing there?"

"I just wanted to see them."

"You stayed awfully late," she narrowed her eyes in suspicion.

I sighed in annoyance.

"The sea otters are disappearing, and the sharks are trying to attack people."

"The sea otters are disappearing? There's only like three thousand of them left on Earth!"

"I know."

"Those animal rights groups are going to have Aqualand's head for this. They're going to think that this is a shoddy aquarium."

On the way back, I had lots of time to think. A lot of things bothered me. Why had the sharks only gone for me? Why were the otters not playful? Why did everyone want to get rid of me so quickly? I decided to say the one thing that bothered me the most.

"What if someone's stealing the otters?" I asked.

"It's possible but I highly doubt it," she sighed, "I'll give it to security."

Then her gaze hardened as she ordered, "Jake do not get involved. Leave this to security."

I nodded.

"Good, now get some rest."

I didn't fall asleep until three in the morning.

I kept thinking about the events that had happened. I wanted to get involved despite Mom's warning. I didn't think the security force was good enough for the case. (Believe it or not, Mad Mary was one of the more competent ones in security.) I recalled the previous night's events multiple times, trying to remember any clues. It got hazier and hazier each time. I was about to give up, but I kept pushing until I found something. I tried for five more minutes and another five minutes. I was about to draw a blank but then I remembered something.

There was a tunnel underneath the otter exhibit. The tunnels went right to an underground viewing area to see the otters swim and play underwater. Somewhere on the wall in that tunnel, there was an employee-only door that blended into the side of the cave-like walls. Inside that employees only door were the employees' offices. There was also a way to get to the hidden part of the otter exhibit.

It was made so that if an otter felt it didn't want to be near a human it could easily swim out of sight. Or in this case scenario, it could also be used to steal otters during tourist hours.

It wasn't much, but it was something.

Chapter 3: Detained

The next morning, I went back to Shark Shallows.

I felt like I missed something important but couldn't figure it out. Although this time when I walked in, the sharks didn't go ballistic. I tried to make sense of it. One day the sharks were trying to attack me and the next day they weren't. As I was mulling that over, Matteo walked up to me.

"Wow you just can't get enough of this place?"

"Do you know why the sharks aren't getting angry at me?" I asked.

"Well, the sharks could have a certain trigger, like a hat or shirt. Even though sharks have poor eyesight they can still remember up to 50 weeks."

"How long ago were the sharks added to Aqualand?"

"About a month."

"That would mean that if they were treated poorly, they would still remember."

"I think you're onto something, Jake. I'll give it to security."

I glanced at my watch; it was 8:55 and school started at 9:00.

"I gotta bolt," I said, then ran off.

I got to school at 9:10. When I walked through the school doors, the principal, Nicolas Casstellio, stormed over.

Mr. Casstellio was tall and overweight. He had a Texas accent and hated kids. He also had a huge temper that was easy to set off.

"So, Jake, late for school huh? I think that's a detention," he snarled.

"That's not fair and you know it," I exclaimed.

Mr. Casstellio did things like that all the time. He accused the wrong kids of the wrong things. In fact, right behind him the school bullies, Spencer Hamilton, Don Wood, and Ron Wood, were mocking him.

Spencer was big and bulky. He got into fights every day and had plenty of bruises and scars. (Although the people who fought him ended up a lot worse.) Ron and Don were twins so dumb, no one could tell them apart, so everyone simply called them RonDon. They were accomplices of Spencer and loved to dish out insults and violence. All of them were eighth graders in the same class as me.

"You're right it's not fair," he said.

I sighed in relief.

"You can stay after school too."

"What!" I gasped, "You can't be serious!"

"Oh, I'm serious all right," he snarled, "now get to class."

I walked into class and sat down next to my best friend, Lander Fields. Lander was short and plump with a huge love for Aqualand. The first day I arrived at Middle Prep Elementary, he came looking for me.

"Dude, where have you been?" he whispered.

"Getting chewed out. I got detention and an after-school punishment for being late."

"When's your detention?"

"During lunch."

He sighed in annoyance; lunch was when he liked to bombard me with questions about Aqualand. It was the only thing he wore, went to, and talked about.

"I think I know who stole the otters. I was going to talk about it during lunch, but I guess that's not going to happen."

I gave him a surprised look and pretended to not know what he meant.

"The otters were stolen?" I asked, playing dumb.

"The otters are vanishing into thin air. I'm pretty sure they can't do that."

"Good point, who do you think it is?"

"Spencer and RonDon."

"Really?" I tried not to sound too dismissive. I was pretty sure it wasn't them. "Why would they want sea otters?"

His grin turned to a frown as he realized he had no reason.

"I didn't think of that. Guess It's not as good of a lead as I thought."

A second after he said that, the bell rang, signaling it was time for lunch. I stood up and started for the office. I was walking for only five minutes before I got into more trouble. The bullies were waiting for me.

And they weren't happy.

Chapter 4: Dumpster Diving

Spencer grabbed the collar of my shirt and slammed me against the wall. Let me just say this now, the whole experience was very painful.

"So, you think we're the otter thieves? Why would we want otters?" Spencer growled.

I tried to say, "I never said that." but it came out as a squeak of air.

"No one accuses us of thievery, let's show him what happens when someone disrespects us," a grin appeared on his face, "take him dumpster diving."

Dumpster diving was the worst thing the bullies could do. They take you to the back of the school and search for the most disgusting dumpster they can find. They then pick you up and shove your face in it for a good twenty seconds. That was happening to me. I was lifted off my feet and carried through the halls. RonDon opened the doors to the backside of the school and then I saw it, the dumpster of doom.

One look at it and I wanted to throw up. It was full of gross, slimy substances. There were some objects I could and couldn't make out. It looked like a few thousand people with a sickness used it as a toilet.

And don't even get me started with the smell.

It smelt like someone took the smell from all the sewer systems in the world and put it into one singular dumpster. I wrinkled my nose in disgust.

"We can talk about this." I was so terrified, just getting those words out was tricky.

"Hmm." Spencer made a show of considering it then he shook his head. "Nah, I think this is more fun."

He flashed me a devilish grin. "Put him in."

I started to get slowly lowered toward the dumpster of doom.

"I can get you behind the scenes in Aqualand." I sputtered making a last-ditch attempt to escape.

"Here's some advice, you should keep your mouth shut unless you want a mouth full of trash," Spencer said with a great amount of menace in his voice. He did have a point, so I closed my mouth and hoped for a miracle.

That miracle was my principal.

I couldn't see what was happening because I was upside down, but I could make out some things. The principal burst through the doors with a lot of force, practically breaking the doors of its hinges. He ranted at me for skipping detention and then telling the bullies to put me down. RonDon didn't put me down because they were still trying to figure out what was happening, but they did loosen their grip on me, which I used to my advantage.

Once I got close enough to the ground, I bent my knees and pushed off as hard as I could toward the dumpster of doom. The force of it sent RonDon flying into Spencer who stumbled under their weight and flew backward with RonDon not far in tow.

Then they fell into the dumpster of doom.

I averted my eyes. Even though their original plan was to do the same to me, it still felt wrong to watch. I could still hear it though. There was a sickening squelch as they hit the filth which was then followed by screams of horror and disgust. When I looked back, the bullies were running away from the school covered in things that I didn't want to think about. (The bullies didn't return to school after that. Even bullies could get embarrassed.)

Mr. Castellio had watched the whole thing and was currently throwing up in a corner. When he was done, he turned back to me. For a second, I saw a hint of fear in his eyes. But only for a second. The anger returned to his eyes and his face turned red.

Then I got suspended.

Otter Ground

Chapter 5: Threatened

I returned home feeling the worst I had ever been.

I'd gotten into trouble on multiple occasions, but it had never been this bad. I had been grounded, yelled at, and kicked out of things many times, but this was worse. A lot worse. First of all, at school, I would be considered a teacher's pet. While most principals suspend bad students, Mr. Castellio suspends good students. Good kids at school were considered the teacher's pets. Second, Mom was going to make sure I didn't get out of her sight until the suspension was over which meant I could no longer investigate. So instead of going home, I went to the otter exhibit.

When I got there, yet another commotion was happening. I walked over to the nearest tourist and asked him what was happening. He simply replied with, "There's only no otters left."

"None left?" I asked incredulously. It seemed hard to believe someone could steal the rest of the otters overnight, but it was still possible.

I pushed through the crowd of humanity and emerged in front of the otter exhibit. Even though I was told what to expect, it still took me by surprise. Every last otter was gone. I peered into the water hoping that at least a few otters were submerged but to my dismay, there wasn't a single sea otter to be seen. As I was searching the water, Mad Mary snuck up behind me and thrust my arms behind my back in an extremely awkward way.

"Returning to the scene of the crime, I see."

She announced it loud enough for most tourists to hear, then she made a show of frisking me for weapons as though I was a dangerous thug instead of a twelve-year-old boy staring at an empty otter exhibit.

"I said this already, I didn't do it," I grumbled, annoyed that I had to go through Mad Mary at the very moment.

"Oh yes you did," she then turned to the crowd of onlookers and announced, "This is the person that stole the very otters you were looking for."

After that last announcement, chaos erupted. People turned to me angrily demanding the otters back while others told Mad Mary that a twelve-year-old boy couldn't make off with twelve otters.

"This boy very much did make off with the otters, I have evidence to prove it! Mad Mary then pulled out an evidence bag. To my and the crowd's surprise the bag contained a few clumps of otter hair.

"I found this in Jake here's trailer. I'm going to take this straight to Aiden River."

The crowd gasped in astonishment, I couldn't form words and Mad Mary looked as happy as I had ever seen her. The very thought of me getting kicked out of Aqualand for something she figured out made her giddy with excitement. Mad Mary pulled out a pair of handcuffs and cupped them onto my arms. There was a distressing click as the handcuffs locked in place. She grabbed my arm and dragged me toward the administration building.

The administration building is where all the important people's offices are. (Although I think that it's for the people that know nothing about aquatic animals.) It was placed on the side of the park right next to the security office. The administration building had 15 different floors for offices. Aiden River's office was on the top floor. When we walked through the doors, the receptionist lady didn't even glance at us. Mad Mary pulled me into an elevator and pressed the button to go to the top floor. There was a small ding and the elevator doors closed.

While we were waiting, I decided to ask, "Why did you search my trailer?"

She shrugged, "Because I did, that's why."

"It seems too smart for an idea of yours," I said, knowing it would get under her skin.

She bristled at the comment.

"I'm not stupid you know. I can have ideas."

I could hardly believe that. Mad Mary had never had an original idea once. (I'd seen her copy what someone else had for lunch then triple it.) Before I could press on, the elevator stopped and the doors opened. There was a small waiting area behind the doors of Aiden River's office. There were two security guards posted outside the doors of the office. Mad Mary brushed past both of them. She pushed through the doors of the office and placed herself in the middle of the room. I entered after her and was immediately taken aback. The office was an extremely large room with an enormous desk near the middle of the room. The desk alone was probably bigger than my trailer. Sitting at that desk was Aiden River.

Aiden River was a short man who looked like he was in his forties. The desk was probably meant to look imposing but all it did was dwarf Aiden. He didn't seem that powerful on the outside, but I could sense superiority, wealth, and power on the inside.

"Jake, just the guy I was looking for." He grinned. (He didn't greet Mad Mary though, which made me feel like I had a chance to defend myself.)

I grinned back, "Pleasure to meet you, sir."

"Please don't call me sir, it's a bit too formal for me." he said.

I nodded.

"I hear you've been investigating the many cases we have going on."

Before I could say anything though, Mad Mary butted in.

"Mr. River, he hasn't been investigating, he's been creating the crimes. I have proof."

She held up the evidence bag and grinned.

"I found this in his trailer last night."

Aiden looked at the bag then at me and then back to the bag.

"You searched Jake's trailer? That doesn't seem like an idea of yours Mary."

Mad Mary recoiled, offended.

"I can have ideas."

I laughed at this. "Did you get this from a source or something because you've never had an idea in your life."

Instead of getting angry like I thought she would, Mad Mary seemed surprised.

"Alright you got me; I got a phone call last night. The caller said that he or she had seen an otter in Jake's trailer. The caller also suggested that I search Jake's place, so I did and found this." She pointed to the bag.

"Who was the caller?" I asked, hoping that Mad Mary wasn't useless.

"I don't know," she said sheepishly. "The caller was anonymous."

I sighed, defeated. Mad Mary was, in fact, useless.

"Alright, let's get back to what I wanted to say," Aiden River said impatiently. "Jake, stop investigating the otter crime."

I couldn't say anything. I was too stunned to talk. First, I was rejected by my own Mom, then the owner of the park.

I felt as though everyone thought I was going to mess everything up because I was a kid. While I was shocked, Mad Mary was excited.

"Jake isn't investigating? Well, now we're going to solve this mystery for sure!"

"Same goes for you, Mary."

With that statement out, Mad Mary's excited exterior cracked like an egg.

"W-well not that I need to investigate because I already caught the criminal." She pointed to me.

"Do you have any more proof because right now, it's all just mere speculation? That bag of evidence would have easily been planted." Aiden said, unconvinced.

He continued, "Do you two understand? No more investigating or I might have to do some things that will affect both of your lives terribly." There was an unsettling amount of menace in his voice.

33

Aiden turned to me. "Let's just say your parents can be replaced. I'm sure other people are willing to take the job."

I gulped.

He moved on to Mad Mary.

"And there are far more competent security officers I can find to take your place."

Mad Mary didn't seem to notice. She was too busy glaring bullets at me. Mad Mary's threat of being fired lightened my mood a bit but not by much. My parents could get fired because of me.

After I had left, my handcuffs had been unlocked which was a huge relief but after the unsettling conversation with Aiden, I was extremely worried. I knew there were cameras everywhere and I feared if I stepped too close to the otter exhibit, my parents' jobs would be as good as gone. (Luckily for me, Aiden didn't know I was investigating the sharks.)

So, I stayed clear of the area and headed home.

When I got home, I found my Mom outside looking slightly terrified as if something had jump-scared her.

That something was a crocodile.

Chapter 6: House Croc

The crocodile surprised me, but not enough to form a scream.

When I saw it, I froze in my tracks, trying my best not to make any sudden movements. This was incredibly stupid though. The thing with animals is that they only attack as a last instinct. Most of the time, they are more scared of humans than we are of them, so when we make a loud noise or move quickly, it activates the animal's attack instincts.

The crocodile wasn't scared of Mom or me. Crocodiles aren't scared of humans like other animals are. (The only animal they are scared of is the hippo.) The crocodile had set himself in an attack position, finding Mom and me as easy prey. If I were to make any sudden movements, I would be animal chow. I started to slowly shuffle towards

Mom. When I arrived, she whispered, "Where have you been?"

"In Aiden River's office," I whispered back, "I was framed."

"Looks like the real thief doesn't like you that much." She pointed to the crocodile. "He put a crocodile in our house for Pete's sake."

I looked back at the crocodile. The trailer was straining under its weight and the walls were creaking ready to fall off. There was a giant hole where the door used to be. The crocodile was about twenty feet long. It weighed what looked like 420 pounds. Mom pulled out her phone and dialed a number.

"Security. What's your business?"

The person on the phone sounded bored.

"There's a crocodile in my house."

"A crocodile?" The person took a long pause, "Sorry, we don't accept prank callers." And with that, the security officer hung up.

"Great," I said bitterly, "Just what we need. We have a crocodile in our house and security thinks we're playing a prank."

"It does sound crazy. A crocodile in someone's house, that's never happened before, why would they believe it?"

Now that she pointed it out, I realized that it did, in fact, sound crazy.

"Well, what do we do now?" I wondered how we would get the crocodile out of the trailer without it breaking.

Only the crocodile solved the problem for me. Just not the way I hoped.

The crocodile suddenly snapped its head upright and started to sniff the air. I did the same thing and found myself breathing in the fumes of fish. As a terrifying jolt of realization hit me, I said, "Mom, you smell like fish."

A little bit of color drained from Mom's face as the crocodile pointed its nose toward us.

"Looks like we figured out how to get the crocodile out of the house," I said.

"Jake, on the count of three, run as fast as you can."

I nodded, planning the opposite of what Mom said.

"One... Two...Three!"

Mom sprinted away as fast as she could. I planted my feet into the ground.

The crocodile noticed the sudden movement and charged after Mom. It was a fact that saltwater crocodiles could run up to twenty-nine miles per hour on land. While my mom ran, I stayed still. It was pretty cool to watch a 406-pound crocodile barrel toward you.

I didn't run because the crocodile was after Mom although, just before it reached me though I dove to the side. I managed to dodge the body but not the tail. The crocodile's tail was flailing around behind him and when I dove it lashed toward me and sent me flying. A crocodile's tail is made of solid muscle. It uses its tail to swim fast or leap out of the water to catch its prey. Or as it turns out, fling twelve-year-old boy thirty-six feet away.

I braced for impact. Every second I was in the air felt like an eternity. It felt so long that I was able to look around. I landed in a bush, which broke my fall. I then looked around and noticed that there was no better time to investigate than now.

So, I headed toward the Otter-torium.

Chapter 7: The Otter Thief

The first thing I did when I got to the Otter-torium was look into the water.

I felt as though I had missed something important. I searched for a few minutes and found nothing.

I was about to go find Mom when from behind, I got pushed into the water. I didn't even know it was happening at first as it had gone so quickly. I fell into the water and sank for a bit until I came to my senses. I kicked my legs and resurfaced. I gulped in some air and climbed out.

It was only then that I noticed that someone was looming over me.

That someone was the Ollie Otter mascot. Ollie Otter was meant for entertainment just like all the other mascots. But this time, instead of him being playful and cute, he looked very menacing, and he had the barrel of a gun pointed at my head! I looked at the gun, considered staying, and then ran away as fast as I could.

A loud bang rang out behind me, Ollie the Otter had fired a shot. It flew past my head and embedded itself in a nearby tree. When Ollie the Otter missed, he sprinted after me. Because he was much bigger and stronger than me, he caught up quickly. Luckily, I knew the park better than him.

I raced past Fishwater Springs and circled around Dolphin Dome. I then ran into the Eel Electricity ride construction site, jumped onto the treads of a bulldozer, grabbed the handle, and climbed onto the roof of it. That was a mistake.

Looking over the edge of the roof, I saw a sickening drop. The bulldozer I was standing on was one of the bigger, stronger types. The average height for a bulldozer was about forty feet. This one looked to be fifty. As I was examining the drop, a second loud bang rang out. It was followed by the sound of something going very fast at the bulldozer, finishing with a metal clang. I looked over the edge and saw that there was a hole the size of a bullet freshly printed on the side of the bulldozer. I then looked back over the edge, considered the drop, and jumped.

I leaped off the side of the bulldozer, hit the ground, and tumbled head over heels. Somehow, I ended up on my feet standing up. I will admit, it was all very impressive. I took a moment to look around and see if anyone saw me but found no one. (There was an owl who saw me, but he didn't look very impressed.) Unfortunately, Ollie, the Otter was climbing down the bulldozer. Very quickly.

I painfully stood up and tried to run away. I now had a limp to my step, so I was going awfully slow. I ran for a few minutes and stopped. I listened for gunshots or footsteps for a moment then slumped against a wall, exhausted. After all the events that had happened, I had a lot of questions.

Is Mom okay? Who is the person in the otter costume?

Why was I being targeted?

I was also annoyed; I had no clue who the thief was despite all my investigating. I also couldn't live at my own house anymore as one of the walls is missing.

I decided to head home and go find Mom.

After a long while of sticking to shadows and keeping my head down, hoping for no more trouble, I found the trailer. Mom was there. She looked exhausted after her run with the crocodile.

"How did you get rid of the crocodile?" I asked.

"I made it chase me until it got tired. I called the crocodile professionals and let them handle it."

"Where are we going to live now?"

"I don't know," Mom said sadly, "I haven't gotten that far yet."

It was getting colder as the sun set for the night and I hadn't put on any warm clothes. I shivered, half because I actually was cold, and half because of the events that had taken place.

"Why don't we talk to Aiden? He could get us a new trailer."

"It's too late out for that. We can just sleep in my office; I can put up an air mattress."

I nodded. Sleeping in a cramped office with an air mattress was still better than sleeping in the trailer. But all in all, I had no house.

Chapter 8: The First Suspect

Mom and I camped out at her office until the next day.

In the morning, we headed toward the administration building. Unlike my last visit, the receptionist lady put up her hand signaling for us to stop. She was on her phone, so we just sat down on a nearby couch and waited.

After a five-minute wait, she finally put down the phone and signaled for us to come over. We stood up and walked over. When we arrived the receptionist lady said, "What do you need?"

Mom and I both replied with, "We need to see Aiden."

"Sure, after all the other thousands of people are finished."

Mom and I had expected this. Aiden had many business deals here along with other random people wanting to talk to Aiden. But when we saw the long line of people waiting for the elevator, we started to realize that even this was unusual. I wondered what was going on. It turned out Mom was thinking the same thing although she put it out, "Why are there so many people wanting to visit him?"

"Well, the head of public relations is there because the tourists want their otters. There's also the shark problem too. He's asking what to say to the public. There's also security. They're just updating him on the ongoing investigation. Lastly, all these businesses that have nothing to do with Aqualand come bumbling along saying that they can fix all Aiden's problems if they pay him, so when I say wait, you know why."

Not long after the receptionist lady said that, the head of PR; (Public Relations) Carl Hills exited, humming a tune. He was a handsome man (all the media pages said so) with a bushy mustache, a square jaw, and a blinding set of white teeth. He always wore a suit and tie. His job, the PR department, is in charge of telling the public what's going on at Aqualand. (Or as it turns out, hiding stuff.) They go on the news to tell the public what's up. They usually talk about the animals which is a little dumb, as their own leader doesn't know squat about them. (He once said that a dolphin is a type of shark.)

When he saw us, he smiled showing a set of perfectly white teeth then said, "Hey, guess what I'm saying to the public! I'm telling them that the otters are hibernating."

I almost immediately knew that wasn't true. Otters do not hibernate. Their fur is warm and thick enough to get them through the winter. Although if he sold it well enough, he could make the public believe that they did indeed hibernate.

The Otter-torium had an underwater section in which the tourists could watch them swim. In the underwater section, there are rooms that the otters can go into to either replenish their breath or avoid tourists. If Carl could sell that they hibernated there, he would be fine until winter ends. Although if anyone were to just simply search up 'do otters hibernate' they would find that it is indeed a sham.

Even though I knew the answer I still decided to ask, "Why cover it up?"

He replied with, "Well, we're not going to tell them the otters were stolen. The animal rights groups would never leave us alone. They would think we're cutting it cheap on animal protection."

"Why would they think that? Aqualand has some pretty good security."

"The animal rights groups think that aquariums are prisons. When they heard the sea otters were vanishing, they blamed us and our security systems."

I hated that there were big groups of people that banded together entirely to bring down aquariums and zoos. Luckily for us, animal rights groups are more focused on zoos as they not only have aquatic animals but also land animals. Not that they leave aquariums alone. They wait outside the gates from opening to closing time, randomly attacking tourists with reasons why aquariums are bad. They also put up flyers on Aqualand's property saying that aquariums are aquatic animal jails.

If that wasn't bad enough, some people actually believed them. All of the people that say or believe that aquariums and zoos are bad are wrong. Scientists believe that in the future, zoos and aquariums will be the only places where animals still exist. Zoos and aquariums are also partial to research on animals. They figure out what causes animal endangerments like habitat loss, global warming, and pollution, all of which are caused by humans, then try to fix them.

As I was thinking that through, someone grabbed me and shoved my arms behind my back. It was too forceful for Mad Mary and the rest of security, so I knew who it was. Blake Morris.

"Jake I believe Aiden told you to stop investigating and what do we find? You swimming in the otter exhibit."

"That wasn't my fault! The crocodile did it!" I said, pleading my innocence. He seemed thrown.

"A crocodile? That's the worst lie I've ever heard. What's next, a guy in an otter costume chasing you with a gun."

"Yes! That's exactly what happened!"

As I said that a slight twinge of suspicion crept up on me. "Wait, how did you know that?"

"Jake, someone tried to kill you?" Mom cut in sounding extremely worried. "Why didn't you tell me?"

"To avoid this reaction."

"Enough of this!" Blake burst out, "Jake, I knew that happened because I have my team searching this week's camera footage."

I knew that was probably true. Aqualand had thousands of cameras hung up. If they actually did find me, they would've found me in about fifteen different shots, which was slightly disconcerting. I still believed that Blake Morris could have been the thief. He had access to security and the supplies to pull off the heist. He was fully capable of stealing eight otters.

I then decided to ask, "Why only the night before?"

Blake rolled his eyes, "Because that's when the rest of the otters were stolen."

I instantly felt dumb for forgetting it. After that sentence, Mad Mary exited the office. Holding handcuffs.

Chapter 9: Short Confrontations

Once again, I had handcuffs on in Aiden River's office.

Except this time, the force against me was pushing harder.

When I entered, Aiden looked angry.

"I told you to stop investigating and I'll tell you again. Jake, stop investigating."

"I did stop investigating!"

"Why were you swimming in the Otter-torium then?"

"I didn't! There was someone dressed in an otter costume. He pushed me in!"

"Someone in an otter costume pushed you?" Aiden chuckled. "Right."

"Sounds like a lame excuse to me." Mad Mary grumbled, "You couldn't possibly believe this. "

"It happened! He also tried to shoot me! If you want proof, go check the side of the bulldozer at the Eel Electricity construction site. There should be a bullet hole there."

Mom then cut in, sounding concerned.

"Someone tried to kill you, Jake? Why didn't you tell me?"

"Because you had the crocodile and the house on your hands. I didn't want you to have any more problems."

"Speaking of the crocodile," Mom said, not sounding as concerned anymore, "We need a new house."

"Why?" Mad Mary and Aiden said at once.

"Because the crocodile broke our wall!" Mom exclaimed.

55

Aiden then got annoyed. It seemed like the thought of spending money, even if it was cheap, was like having a dolphin spit at him. Multiple times.

He hesitated for too long for Mom, so she said, "I guess you'll have to find a new fish expert." That was enough to make Aiden crack. "Fine, I'll have you a new trailer by tomorrow."

"I'd like a double wide please."

"What!" He gasped, "I can't do that! Then everyone else would want one."

Mom shrugged, "Start counting your bills then."

Aiden River, the ruthless businessman and master of negotiating, knew he couldn't win. Or at least he couldn't win if he didn't want all his workers to quit. He seemed to age a few years as he rubbed his temples. He no longer seemed annoyed so much as confused.

"Fine, now could you folks leave? Y'all are giving me a migraine."

We all exited the office. Mom was happy that we were getting an upgraded home while Mad Mary was angry that things didn't go her way. Meanwhile, my mind was whirring with thoughts like, why did Aiden want me to stop investigating so badly?

Was he hiding something? Should I look into Blake?

How did he know about the otter guy so quickly? There were over 100 hours of footage;   his security wouldn't have been able to find me that fast. I had my suspicions about Blake and Aiden and there was no way I was going to stop investigating.

I would've headed home if I had one, but I didn't. It was past closing time in Aqualand, and the sun was setting. I was on edge. Every time I heard a loud noise or a shadow shift, I would flinch. I knew I was being paranoid but, in my defense, I was almost killed. So, this time instead of heading to the Otter-torium I went to Shark Shallows.

Shark Shallows is very creepy during sunset. The glow of the setting sun illuminated the sharks in an unnerving way. The sharks were also back to staring at me, trying to get through the glass and eating me. This made them even more creepy. I pulled out my phone and turned on its light using it to see my surroundings better. Everything appeared normal, trash strewn everywhere, stained floors, and an open employee door.

I must've been getting sleepy because it took me a few seconds to figure out that an open employee door isn't normal. I was suddenly wide awake. At that point, I noticed many other things. There were glass shavings, the glass for the sharks were tinted with red, and there was now a hand on my shoulder. "What are you doing here?" someone grumbled in my ear.

The telltale sound of Blake Morris.

"I came to see the sharks," I said, trying to sound calm. Instead, I was excited. I was excited because I had almost solved the case. There was one more thing I needed to find out. Luckily, Blake did just what I wanted.

He grabbed me by the arm and angrily said, "Jake come with me to my office."

A few minutes later, I found myself sitting in Blake's office. Blake's office was found in the security building. The security building was right next to the administration building. It was a big structure but was still dwarfed by the administration building. The security building consisted of a front lobby and three different long hallways of offices. At the end of two of the hallways, they connected into a large room. The large room was just a massive coffee shop. (It turned out some of the security officers only joined because of the coffee shop.) At the end of the last hallway was Blake's office, which was where we sat now.

Blake's office was small but bigger than the others. It had a closet, a small desk, and two chairs. And just as I had wanted, I found tinted red shavings of glass on the ground. I also noticed a can of red paint. The name of the company was 'Bloody Red Paint' and it advertised that it had the smell of blood. (It also said it was perfect haunted house material.) By that point, I knew who messed with the sharks' temperament. Blake Morris had been caught.

Well, he was still free until I got out of his office but I knew it was him. Blake seemed to realize that too.

 "Listen, this stuff isn't mine. I found it here this morning out of nowhere. Don't go off telling everyone. I don't want to hurt you."

The last thing he said made me go on guard. I noticed that the door was locked which also made me on edge. I locked eyes with him and said "Fine, I won't tell anyone."

Blake seemed satisfied.

"Alright but tell anyone and I'll have to use force to shut you up."

With that, he stood up, walked to the door, unlocked it, and held it open. "Go home."

I exited the office and returned to Mom's office wanting nothing more but sleep.

I returned to Mom's office to find that it was gone.

The office looked as though it had been pulled right out from the rest. Dr. Peterson, Mom's fellow fish researcher, had his office right next to hers. He was now missing a wall. But that wasn't nearly as bad as a missing office. Mom's office was right in the corner of the building. It now looked like someone had cut the corner off the building as though it were a slice of cake. You could also see a bit of the top of the huge fish tank inside Fishwater Springs. The researchers for the fish viewed from above on a viewing platform. I was so exhausted that even the viewing platform looked comfy. So, with that Mom and I were stuck sleeping on the floor on top of a fish tank. We had the cold floor, a cold night breeze, and no warm clothes. I had been threatened, handcuffed, and ignored.

So, to sum it up, it was a really crummy day.

Chapter 10: Broken

I forgot all about Blake's villandry.

I was planning to tell Mom that Blake was the bad guy, but I unfortunately forgot. I was more focused on the otters. It still seemed crazy that overnight, a raft of otters could be stolen. (A raft of otters is a group of otters.) I didn't feel like going to the Otter-torium because I had almost been killed. I ended up wandering around the park looking for clues. During which I ran into Mad Mary.

"Trying to act innocent today? I'm onto you." She grabbed my arm.

"I'm just wandering around and yet you still try to take me down. That's pretty pathetic, even for you."

She took that in for a second then shook her head. Not much could get through her thick skull.

"I don't believe you one bit. You're trouble and a kid. Of course, you were the villain. All kids should not be trusted."

"You know who you are? You're a bully. No matter, what you want to take me down. You target me specifically only because I'm smaller than you. That's what bullies do."

I had never thought of Mad Mary this way before but as I said it, I realized I was right. Mad Mary seemed stunned that I had put that statement out. She opened her mouth as if to say something, but nothing came out. Then her head turned as red as a baboon's butt.

"That's it, you want to investigate? Fine." Mad Mary fumed, "Come on, smart guy, we don't have all day." And with that, she dragged me to Shark Shallows

Once we entered the giant glass dome, Mad Mary released her grasp on my arm.

"Go on, know it all, investigate."

I moved around the room and searched every corner and under every bench. The whole time, Mad Mary kept a steely stare on me. It was very unnerving which made it hard to focus. After three minutes of searching, Mad Mary got impatient.

"Found anything yet?"

"Yeah, the sharks aren't acting up," I said, showing the most sarcasm I possibly could.

That was a lie, the sharks were still making a ruckus. I also had noticed a few things like the glass was slightly tinted red and there was a dry, metallic smell. I knew this smell but couldn't figure out what it was.

"Do you smell that?" I asked.

Mad Mary inhaled deeply and then said, completely oblivious to her own stench, "I don't smell anything."

"Oh well, never mind."

Just as I said that, an alarm went off and some metal doors slammed shut on all the exits. I then noticed something even more alarming than the alarm and metal doors; there was a stick of C4 wedged into the glass.

The sharks suddenly seemed ten times more terrifying than before. Aqualand had one maneater shark out of the dozen species of man eaters: the Shortfin Mako Shark. The Shortfin Mako has had one human fatality and harmed eight more. All happened because they were protecting their territory. We were about to get forced into their territory. The C4 beeped and then exploded. Cracks slowly spread through the glass, breaking the separation between Mad Mary, the sharks and me. I glanced at Mad Mary who had become paralyzed and pale as she watched the glass break. I took a deep breath and braced for impact.

The next thing I knew, the glass shattered.

Chapter 11: Sunk

Being stuck in a shark tank that had just exploded made the top list of bad things that had happened to me so far.

First, there was the impact of the icy cold water being thrown down on me, then the fact that I had to avoid the glass shards and finally, the sharks themselves.

The water came down like a truck, knocking all the energy out of me. Once the impact stopped, I kicked upwards as hard as I could toward the top of the glass dome that was slowly breaking apart, because there was an air pocket up there and an emergency exit. Something brushed past my leg. It was the Mako shark, and it didn't look happy. Makos are extremely protective of their territory so that meant that I was in danger. (More than I already was.)

Right then, I suddenly remember Dad telling me, *"If you ever encounter a shark, punch it in the nose."*

So, I pulled my arm back, clenched my hand into a fist and punched the shark square in the nose. It whimpered and swam away. Its tail knocked against my skin and a fresh wound opened up for saltwater to rush in. It stung like crazy! By that point, I was running out of breath but, luckily, I was almost to the top of the water.

I breached the waterline and took in as much air as I could. As the water cleared out of my brain, I realized Mad Mary wasn't with me. Without thinking, I took a deep breath and went back underwater.

I found Mad Mary flailing about, face slowly turning darker shades of purple. I swam to her, grabbed one of her arms and kicked upward. We resurfaced and Mad Mary promptly passed out. I took the walkie talkie that she had in one of her belt pockets and pressed the button.

"Uh, we need all available personnel immediately at Shark Shallows. The tank blew up and Mary and I are stuck in it. (I had heard Mad Mary say stuff like this before but it's usually not about the shark tank but about me instead.)

"All available personnel are on the way." said the woman on the other side of the walkie talkie.

I stayed in my spot, treading water for the next three minutes while holding Mad Mary and anxiously watching the cracks spread farther and farther down the dome. I'll just say it was exhausting. I didn't use the emergency exit because I couldn't haul Mad Mary up the ladder with me. Eventually we got out of there.

Mad Mary, who had woken up, seemed embarrassed by the whole ordeal. Many towels and blankets had been wrapped around us, but we were still shivering like crazy. Every part of my body felt numb. Then at that moment there was a loud shattering noise, and everyone snapped their heads towards it.

Shark Shallows had collapsed.

Chapter 12: Trapped

The first thing I did in the morning was tell Mom that Blake was the one who gave the sharks their undying anger.

I remembered it as Shark Shallows had collapsed. Mom probably wouldn't appreciate me continuing to investigate but I needed to tell someone of my discovery.

Although it turned out that I didn't need to worry about being chastised. To my surprise, she was interested. As I explained my theory, Mom listened intently. I told her everything from going to Shark Shallows to the blood paint. Once I was finished, Mom asked, "You said that Blake told you that the evidence was planted? He could be telling the truth, after all, you said it was pretty obvious."

"It's possible," I admitted.

71

"Looks like we still need to find that out before we have a full case."

I sighed, despite all my investigating, I still needed to uncover more. Blake could be faking the planted evidence, or he could've planted the evidence and said that the thief planted it to throw me off his trail. And despite all that, I still had to figure out who the otter thief was. I knew it was a lot to place the burden of figuring out both cases without help on myself, but I had felt strangely excited to investigate. I was so close, and I wasn't going to give up.

So, with that, I excused myself and headed toward the Otter-torium.

Of course, I was being careful about it. To disguise myself, I dressed up in Aqualand merchandise.

Mom had crappy pay. Although Mom didn't expect pay, she accepted the job to research fish, not for money. We got a little bit below one hundred dollars per day and every month we got our casual pay along with one free Aqualand merchandise piece. We got things like T-shirts, pants, bathing suits, underwear, and caps. There was a bin in our house full of Aqualand's merchandise. I used pants, T-shirts, underwear, and caps to my advantage. (Aiden had asked many times why the underwear wasn't getting many sales. I had figured out why. It was very uncomfortable and scratchy.) I had an Aqualand cap pulled over my eyes that had a corny message on it: 'Water you waiting for? Get out there!' I had an Aqualand shirt with Sally Shark on it saying 'We don't bite! Come for a visit!'

My pants had one dolphin on each leg. I had also invited Lander as I would be more disguised with a friend. It also helped to have an extra pair of eyes.

Unlike the last time I saw the Otter-torium, there was no crowd. It seemed as though the tourists had gotten bored of looking into the empty vastness of the water and left. I now had a clear, open view of the water. Lander and I scanned the water for a few minutes. Lander reported that he hadn't seen anything. I hadn't either. Before we left to go search the rest of the Otter-torium I glanced at the water one more time. A small glint caught my eye and what I noticed was not what I expected.

The metal ring of a trapdoor handle.

It was right in the middle of the otter's pond and if I wanted to get to it, I had to go for a swim.

"Look," I pointed to the trapdoor, "there's a trapdoor over there."

Lander looked at where I was pointing and quickly found out what I wanted to do.

"Oh no, I am not doing that."

"Alright, I'll do it. But I'll never let you forget about this."

"Fine, I'm coming," he grumbled, not wanting me to tease him.

And with that, we pulled off our shirts and vaulted over the rope into the water. Although we had taken a second to make sure we wouldn't hit any rocks.

As I flew through the air, I noticed that the trapdoor could be for something completely useless and we were doing something extremely reckless. But of course, it was too late to turn back. I stuck my arms to my sides and put my legs together. I made sure to point my toes as not doing so would break my feet from the impact. Lander wasn't as clean as me and bellyflopped into the water with a painful smack.

We hit the water cleanly and shot downward. I resurfaced a bit before Lander. A few seconds passed before he surfaced beside me, gasping for breath. By the time he pulled his head out of the water, I was nearly to the trapdoor. He paddled after me and came to my side. I was looking at the trapdoor that was now right underneath us. Then I ducked my head under the water and swam downwards. I reached the trapdoor and pulled on the handle which was much heavier than I expected. Lander joined me and together we pulled the trapdoor upward.

Both of us looked in and found a ladder leading downward. We swam in and, after a very tiring while, managed to shut it again. The water drained out of the room and onto the ground. We both gulped in air.

I climbed down the ladder hand by hand-with Lander not far behind. We emerged into a slightly damp room with a giant window. The room had a large desk with computers on top of it near the farthest wall we were standing from. Each computer had security camera clips on them. And in the far corner sat a medium-sized holding cell.

In that holding cell were the otters.

Unfortunately for us, a man was standing in our way.

And he had guns pointed at our heads.

Chapter 13: Case Closed

I was now stuck in a cramped room with a gun pointed at my head.

Frankly, I was getting tired of having deadly threats to my wellbeing and my life and right now I was being threatened just before I retrieved the otters. It was very annoying at how close I had come only to fail in the end.

The guns looked even more menacing with the dim light - the glimmer of the gun, and the bullet loaded inside the barrel of the gun. Lander beside me was trembling in fear, meanwhile, to my surprise, I was oddly calm in this circumstance, you could even say I was a bit excited. I took a second to look at the man in front of us and noticed that he was dressed from head to toe in black. A ski mask covered his face, and he wore a slick, black outfit. The only reason I knew it was a man was because of the bushy mustache outline behind the mask.

At that moment I was struck with a realization.

"I think I know who the otter thief is," I whispered to Lander.

"Who?"

"C-"

I couldn't finish my sentence because Mad Mary suddenly burst into the room and tackled the man. They tumbled onto the floor and rolled around fighting for the guns. (I will admit I was a little impressed by Mad Mary's sudden heroics.) They shifted into a position where the man could launch Mad Mary off him, which is exactly what he did.

In one powerful movement of his legs, he managed to fling Mad Mary off him and once again get control of the gun.

And then, he shot himself in the foot.

It turned out there were only sedatives loaded in the gun and they worked rather fast. Within seconds, our ambusher had retrieved the guns, shot himself, and collapsed to the floor with a thud. I found the whole situation ironic. Mad Mary got up with a struggle and gave the man a slight nudge with her foot to make sure he was out for good. I approached the sack of otters and untied it. I found all twelve sea otters crammed against each other in a heap. They didn't look good after spending four days in a bag. They had patches of fur missing and were so tired when I picked one up it didn't even fight back, it just fell asleep in my arms.

"Mad Mary," I said, "can you take the otters back to their home?"

"Sure." With that, Mad Mary pulled the otters out of the bag and climbed up the ladder. We followed behind her and after a bit, exited the damp room.

Once we were out of the water I decided to ask, "Mad Mary, how did you find us?"

"I was tailing you. I figured you were up to no good."

"Well, thanks for saving us."

I figured I owed her an apology as she had just saved our butts. Lander quickly chimed in with his apology as well.

Mad Mary laughed, "Save you? You were clearly working with the bad guy. I didn't do that to save you, I did it to arrest you."

Lander and I both gaped at her in shock. It turned out Mad Mary's thick skull was oblivious to the fact that we had just been threatened with guns. Luckily for me, I knew who the real culprit was although I didn't have much evidence to prove my case. Mad Mary, on the other hand, had caught me slinking around the Otter-torium and entering a suspicious room. So, with that Mad Mary pulled out two pairs of handcuffs and locked them to Lander and my wrists.

It was now the third time that I was wearing handcuffs, heading to Aiden's office.

Once we arrived at the administration building, Mad Mary rushed us inside and breezed past the receptionist lady, despite her many protests and warnings. We stepped into the elevator and after an awkward pause, burst out of the elevator and headed toward Aiden's office. We heard talking from the inside and what I heard was astonishing. I pressed my ear up against the door and heard Aiden say, "When's construction starting?"

I then heard Blake reply, "Soon, the explosives did the trick, Shark Shallows is in shambles!"

"Yeah. So, do you think the glass slide will get more tourists?"

I didn't get to hear anymore because Mad Mary suddenly burst through the door, dragging Lander and me behind her.

"I know who the otter thieves are!" Mad Mary announced it so loud her voice echoed off the walls.

Aiden and Blake both reacted in two different ways. Blake became angry demanding to know why we had interrupted their meeting and Aiden was skittish.

"Um… Er… Who?" Aiden seemed like he had just been surrounded by a shiver of sharks. (A shiver of sharks is what you call a pack of sharks as most people shiver when a group of sharks is nearby.)

"Thieves? Plural?" Blake said.

"Jake and his little friend!" Mad Mary exclaimed it so happily I half expected her to start bouncing off the walls.

"No," Lander protested, "it was…" He looked at me.

"It was Carl," I said, finishing his sentence.

"That's… Er… Very good."

Aiden glanced at the closed bathroom door.

"Now could you… Er… leave? I'm… Um… in the middle of… Er… a very important meeting."

At that moment, a cheerful man emerged from the bathroom and said, "Alright I'm ready to start the construction on Shark Shallows and…" He stopped talking when Blake shot him a warning glare.

"Hey," Mad Mary said, finally realizing something was up, "What's going on?"

"Um… Er…" Aiden couldn't even form words as he was so nervous.

"Oh!" The cheerful man said gleefully, "Aiden had once announced that he wanted to rebuild Shark Shallows and the tourists didn't like that. Aiden still wanted to rebuild though, and he needed an excuse that wouldn't make him lose business so he hired Blake. Blake swapped the normal glass, rather professionally I must say, with blood glass. All the sharks got angry and started attacking the glass.

But it didn't look that way to the tourists. They thought the sharks were going after them which scared them off. Aiden told the public that the structure of Shark Shallows caused it and it needed to be rebuilt. Aiden then hired me and my crew to start construction which is why I'm here."

Aiden and Blake both glared at the man.

"Wow, thanks a lot." they said at once.

"Um," I said, "I solved the case of the missing sea otters."

"No," Aiden said menacingly looking at Lander and me, "Mary solved the case. I'm sending you two off to juvie."

"What! But we didn't do it! Jake found the real thief! Didn't you hear him? It's Carl, not us!" Lander was sweating profusely.

"Oh?" Aiden taunted, "And what's your evidence?"

"We found a trapdoor in the Otter-torium. It took both of us to open and close it. When we got in there was a man dressed in all black with a ski mask over his head. Poking out of that ski mask was a bushy mustache. Carl's mustache. Now, quick question, how long was Carl gone for when he set out to make the excuse to the public?"

"3 hours." The cheerful man said.

"It shouldn't have been that long. All he needed to do was say the otters were hibernating, right? It took Lander and me five minutes to get the trapdoor open and the same amount of time to close it. So, it would've taken a while for Carl. He also made the announcement an hour and a half before closing time, so he needed to wait for the tourists to clear out, to get into the room and don't forget about feeding the otters which for the employees here usually takes half an hour, which is why he was gone so long."

Everyone in the room paused, taking that in.

Then Aiden laughed and said, "Is that all you got? A mustache and a trapdoor? That was one lame excuse."

The cheerful man's enthusiasm dropped a few notches, "No it's true, Carl is the otter thief. He wanted revenge on the park for docking his pay and I found out. He said that if I told anyone he would find out."

Everyone paused once again.

"So… case closed?" Lander said.

"I guess so," Blake said. Aiden looked to Mad Mary, Lander, and me.

"Can you folks not say anything about the project? I want this new Shark Shallows built. It'll be really cool, trust me. It's gonna have a glass slide that goes through the shark tank, it'll have a second floor so you can view from above and a restaurant. Trust me you'll want it."

Lander and I nodded. Mad Mary still seemed to be taking in my case, trying to find a good argument. Her face was scrunched up in thought.

"Alright, could you folks leave? I need to be ready to rebuild."

With that, we cleared out of the office and headed home.

Both cases had been solved and I had returned home feeling proud.

After all, I solved the otter case.

Chapter 14: Epilogue

I looked over the railing to get a glimpse of the baby sea otters.

Doc had called us almost immediately to come down because of the brand-new baby sea otters. Even Aiden showed up to see them as sea otters are endangered.

Doc had said, "When I let you in, do not interrupt the mother and baby. Don't make noise, just watch, okay?"

We had all chimed in our agreements.

We were on the rope bridge looking at the baby sea otters. As I watched them play with their mom, I thought about all the work that had gone into saving those poor sea otters. I had to investigate day and night, narrow down possible subjects and go through many life-threatening attacks to find the thief. Come to think of it, I went through angry sharks, bullies, a house croc, a confrontation with the otter thief, a stolen office, the collapse of Shark Shallows, and the trapdoor. When I think about it, there was a lot of danger that had happened in the last five days. I was lucky to survive all those encounters, and Mad Mary turned out to be an incredibly stupid hero.

It wrapped up with Carl, the clueless head of PR that stole all the otters. The angry sharks turned out to be ticked off because of blood glass all because Aiden River was scared that the public would be angry that Shark Shallows would be closed. All in all, the dangerous times were all caused by, and for, stupid reasons.

The END